SHORT TALES
Fairy Tales

The Little Mermaid

Adapted by Gary Reed
Illustrated by Bill Bryant

WAYLAND

WAYLAND

First published in 2013 by Wayland

Copyright © 2013 Wayland

Wayland
338 Euston Road
London NW1 3BH

Wayland Australia
Level 17/207 Kent Street
Sydney, NSW 2000

All Rights Reserved.

Adapted Text by Gary Reed
Illustrations by Bill Bryant
Colours by Wes Hartman
Edited by Stephanie Hedlund
Interior Layout by Kristen Fitzner Denton and Alyssa Peacock
Book Design and Packaging by Shannon Eric Denton
Cover Design by Alyssa Peacock

Copyright © 2008 by Abdo Consulting Group

A cataloguing record for this title is available at the British Library.
Dewey number: 823.9'2

Printed in China

ISBN: 978 0 7502 7753 2

Wayland is a division of Hachette Children's Books, an Hachette UK company.
www.hachette.co.uk

Far out in the deep blue sea was the castle of the Sea King.

The Sea King had six beautiful daughters.

When the girls turned 16 years old, they were allowed to go to the surface.

There, they could see people who didn't have fins.

Soon, all of the girls had been to the surface except for the youngest.

She was the Little Mermaid.

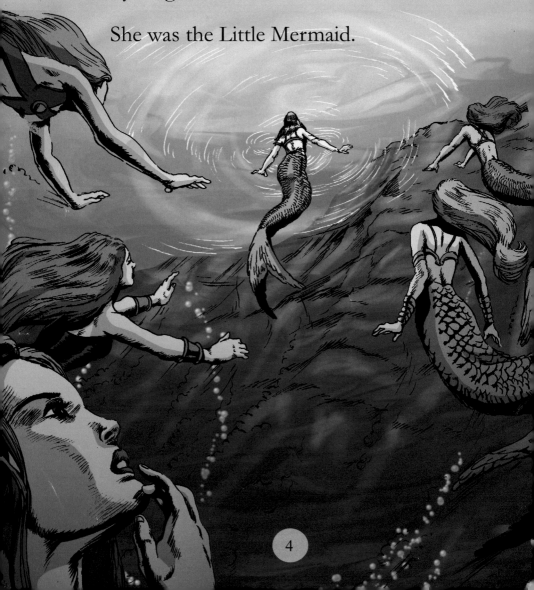

At last the Little Mermaid's day came.

When she rose out of the water, she saw a ship.

The Little Mermaid didn't want to get too close,
but she heard music.

She swam closer so she could see the people better.

There was a handsome Prince on board. The party was for the Prince.

The Little Mermaid didn't want to go back home.

Night came and the skies turned dark.

The Little Mermaid saw the moon for the first time.

Then it was blocked by a black cloud.

She jumped when a flash of lightning came.

She was about to go home again, but lightning struck the Prince's ship.

The ship caught fire.

The brave Prince began helping others to get off the burning ship.

Then the mast fell over and struck him.

The Little Mermaid saw the Prince fall into the water.

She swam to find him.

When she did, she pulled him up to the surface.

Then she swam to the shore, with the Prince in her arms.

As she rested his head on the sand, she sang him a song.

She knew she should leave, but she wanted to stay.

The Little Mermaid brushed the hair from his face.

The Prince opened his eyes.

'Are you an angel?' he asked her.

The Little Mermaid shook her head and said 'No.'

The Prince closed his eyes again.

'You sound like an angel to me' he said.

She bent down and kissed him.

The Little Mermaid heard people coming.

They had seen her bring the Prince to shore.

They were still far away, so they didn't know she was a mermaid.

She slipped away before they got too close.

When they had gone, the Little Mermaid
returned home.

She told her sisters of the wonderful Prince.

They reminded her that mermaids and humans
could not live together.

But the Little Mermaid knew there was someone who could help her.

She swam to the dark water and found the mean Sea Witch.

The plants around her house tried to grab the Little Mermaid as she swam by!

As the Little Mermaid came to the house, the Sea Witch opened the door.

'I know why you are here' the Sea Witch said.

'I can give you legs and make you human for one year' she said.

'If the Prince marries you, then you will stay human' she said. 'If not, then you will die.'

15

The Little Mermaid was scared, but tried not to show it.

'What do I have to do?' she asked the Sea Witch.

'You have to pay my price' the Sea Witch said.

'What do you want?' the mermaid asked.

'Your voice' said the Sea Witch. 'Your beautiful voice.'

The Little Mermaid was shocked.

How could she sing to the Prince without her voice?

'If you do not think the Prince will love you, then go and leave me alone' the Sea Witch said, moving away.

'Okay. I'll do it' the Little Mermaid said.

The Sea Witch turned to the Little Mermaid.

In her hand was a cup full of something green.

'Drink this, and your wish will come true' said the witch.

The Little Mermaid drank it. It tasted horrible.

But now she could be with her Prince.

Soon, the Little Mermaid woke up.

She was not in the water but on the beach!

The last thing she remembered was drinking the green potion.

She had an even bigger surprise when she looked down.

Her fin was gone. Now she had legs!

Then she heard people coming towards her.

At the front was the Prince!

She stood up to greet them but fell down again.

The Prince helped her up.

He asked her who she was.

The Little Mermaid wanted to tell him that she was
the one who had saved his life.

But when she opened her mouth, nothing came out.

Then she remembered: the Sea Witch had
her voice.

The Prince led her towards his palace.

He kept looking at her as if he knew her.

Finally, he said that she looked like an angel he saw once.

But that angel sang a beautiful song, so it couldn't be her.

'I must get married in the next year' said the Prince.
'But I don't know any girls that I can talk to.'

The Little Mermaid smiled and pointed to herself.

The Prince laughed.

'Good!' he said. 'Then you will stay here and teach
me about girls.'

So the Little Mermaid stayed with the Prince.

They took long walks together and rode horses.

They became great friends.

One day the Prince took the Little Mermaid for a carriage ride.

He told her that he had to visit the Princess that he was to marry.

He was sad. He wanted to marry a friend like her, but his bride must be a Princess.

The Little Mermaid could not tell him that her father was the Sea King. So she was also a princess!

When the Prince returned, he wasn't sad anymore.

He had met the Princess and she was wonderful.

The Little Mermaid knew the Prince had fallen in love with her.

That night, the Little Mermaid stood on the beach.

The year was up and she was not going to marry the Prince.

That meant she was going to die.

Then she heard her sisters calling her.

Her sisters told her the Sea Witch would let her live.

But she had to cut off the hair of the Princess and give it to the witch.

The Little Mermaid said she would not do that.

'Then you will die when the sun comes up' her sisters said.

And with sadness, they went back into the water.

The sun came up as the year ended.

Then three girls floated down from the clouds.

They were angels who watched over people.

They told the Little Mermaid that she was to join them.

'Your heart is pure and you have done good deeds' one of them said.

'So you are to become one of us' another said.

They reached out their hands for her.

The Little Mermaid floated up in the air.

She had lived in water and on land.

Now she was to live in the air.

She could go anywhere the wind took her.

The Little Mermaid floated over the sleeping Prince and kissed him on the cheek.

She sang a song to him. Even though he was asleep, she saw that he smiled.

SHORT TALES
Fables

Titles in the Short Tales Fables series:

The Ants and the Grasshopper

978 0 7502 7756 3

The Boy Who Cried Wolf

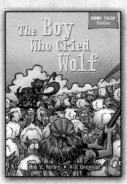

978 0 7502 7757 0

The Fox and the Grapes

978 0 7502 7758 7

The Lion and the Mouse

978 0 7502 7783 9

The Tortoise and the Hare

978 0 7502 7784 6

The Town Mouse and the Country Mouse

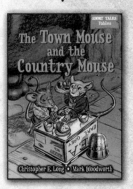

978 0 7502 7785 3

WAYLAND

www.waylandbooks.co.uk

Follow us on Twitter @waylandbooks | Find us on Facebook Wayland Books

SHORT TALES
Fairy Tales

Titles in the Short Tales Fairy Tales series:

Aladdin and the Lamp

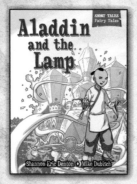

978 0 7502 7750 1

Beauty and the Beast

978 0 7502 7752 5

Jack and the Beanstalk

978 0 7502 7751 8

Puss in Boots

978 0 7502 7754 9

Sleeping Beauty

978 0 7502 7755 6

The Little Mermaid

978 0 7502 7753 2

WAYLAND

www.waylandbooks.co.uk

Follow us on Twitter @waylandbooks | Find us on Facebook Wayland Books